A Big Decision

"I wonder what time Mr. Quincy's coming to pick up Joe," Jessica said. "He could be at our house right now. I hope he's gone before we get home."

Elizabeth felt pangs of guilt as she imagined her parents confronting an irate Mr. Quincy. "I wish we could hang around here, but I really think we should be home before he comes. What are we going to say to him about Joe?"

"We'll say he ran away," Jessica replied. "There's no way Mr. Quincy can prove he didn't."

Elizabeth felt uncomfortable at the thought of lying, especially in front of her parents.

But then she looked at Joe. Even though the dog's physical appearance was pretty peculiar, his cuts had healed and he was acting like a normal dog. Maybe it was worth lying to see him so happy.

SWEET VALLEY TWINS

Teamwork

Written by
Jamie Suzanne

Created by
FRANCINE PASCAL

A BANTAM SKYLARK BOOK®
TORONTO • NEW YORK • LONDON • SYDNEY • AUCKLAND

To Briana Ferris Adler

RL 4, 008–012

TEAMWORK
A Bantam Skylark Book / March 1989

Sweet Valley High® and Sweet Valley Twins are trademarks of
Francine Pascal

Conceived by Francine Pascal.

Cover art by James Mathewuse.

Produced by Daniel Weiss Associates, Inc.,
27 West 20th Street, New York, NY 10011

Skylark Books is a registered trademark of Bantam Books, a division of
Bantam Doubleday Dell Publishing Group, Inc.
Registered in U.S. Patent and Trademark Office and elsewhere.

ISBN 0-553-15681-0

Published simultaneously in the United States and Canada

Bantam Books are published by Bantam Books, a division of Bantam
Doubleday Dell Publishing Group, Inc. Its trademark, consisting of
the words "Bantam Books" and the portrayal of a rooster, is Registered
in U.S. Patent and Trademark Office and in other countries. Marca
Registrada. Bantam Books, 666 Fifth Avenue, New York, New York 10103.

PRINTED IN THE UNITED STATES OF AMERICA

O   0 9 8 7 6 5 4 3 2

One

◇

"Look what I found!" Jessica Wakefield said as she burst into her twin sister Elizabeth's room on a rainy Sunday afternoon. She pointed to an advertisement in a magazine. "Isn't this neat?"

It was an ad for crystal glassware, and the photograph showed a group of people seated at a dining room table offering a toast. The women were wearing elegant long gowns and lots of decorative jewelry, while the men wore dark suits. The table was covered with a lace cloth, sparkling crystal and china, and a huge arrangement of flowers between two fancy candlesticks.

"It's pretty," Elizabeth said. "Sort of romantic-looking." She was curled up on her bed with a French cookbook she had found in the kitchen.

Jessica sat down on the edge of Elizabeth's bed and gazed at the advertisement with dreamy eyes. "I wish I could dress up like this and go to a fancy dinner. Just think, Elizabeth, soft music, candlelight, dancing with an incredibly cute boy . . . wouldn't it be wonderful?"

Elizabeth grinned. Jessica's daydreams usually centered around clothing and boys, whereas Elizabeth dreamed about winning blue ribbons in a horse show or having her writing published in a magazine.

It wasn't really strange that Elizabeth's fantasies were so different from Jessica's. The twins were complete opposites in every way—except for their appearance. They both had long blond hair, blue-green eyes, and a dimple in their left cheeks. But that's where the similarities ended.

Elizabeth was the more serious of the two. She liked being with her friends and having good talks, but she also enjoyed spending time alone, reading and writing and sometimes just thinking about things.

Jessica, on the other hand, spent most of her time with a group of friends who were always getting involved in some kind of complicated scheme. She was a member of the Unicorn Club, made up of the most popular Sweet Valley Middle School girls who thought they were as special as the mythical beast after which their club was named. They had even chosen purple—the color of royalty —as the club's official color. As far as Elizabeth could tell, there was nothing special about them. She had nicknamed them the Snob Squad because all they ever did was talk about clothes, other girls, and boys.

Right now, however, Jessica was staring glumly out the window. "I wish the rain would stop. It's so boring hanging around at home." She tossed the magazine aside and fell back on Elizabeth's bed. "I want to do something—something different."

Elizabeth looked at her sister sympathetically. "Well, maybe we could cook something. Listen to this." She read from her cookbook. "Delicately seasoned chicken breasts wrapped around paper-thin slices of cheese and ham, sauteed in herb butter, and covered with a light cream sauce. Doesn't that sound delicious?"

Jessica stared at the ceiling. "Mmm."

"And look at this." Elizabeth held the book up for Jessica to see.

Jessica's face went sour as she read from the page. "Chocolate *mouse*? That's disgusting!"

"I think it's pronounced *moose*." Elizabeth giggled. "Chocolate mousse is sort of like pudding, but fancier."

Jessica sighed wistfully. "I'll bet that's the kind of food people eat at elegant dinner parties."

Elizabeth studied the recipe for a moment. "You know, Jess, this really looks easy to make."

Jessica sat up abruptly. "That's it!"

Elizabeth looked at her in confusion. *"What's* it?"

"We could have a dinner party! *That* would be something different to do." She turned excitedly to her sister. "We'll invite some friends, and tell them they have to get dressed up in fancy clothes. And we'll get Mom to let us use her best china and her crystal goblets. We'll make the chicken recipe, and that chocolate mousse, too."

Elizabeth looked at her sister doubtfully. If they really did have a dinner party, she thought, she would end up doing most of the work. Even so, the idea began to sound exciting. "That might be fun. I could invite Amy and Nora and Julie." Amy Sutton, Nora Mercandy, and Julie Porter were Elizabeth's closest friends. "Amy might not like the idea of dressing up, though," she added.

"Amy will have to wear a dress," Jessica said firmly. "We'll make that a rule. And I'll invite the Unicorns."

"All of them?" Elizabeth asked. "That's a lot of chocolate mousse!"

"Well, maybe just Lila Fowler and Ellen Riteman then, and . . . wait a minute!" Now her eyes began to sparkle. "We should invite some boys, too."

"Boys?"

"Sure! One boy for each girl. And they'll have to wear suits." Jessica opened the magazine again. "It'll be just like in this picture."

Elizabeth studied the picture more closely. "I don't know," she said doubtfully. She thought it would be even harder to get the boys into suits than it would be to get Amy into a fancy dress.

"Maybe we should invite a few more people." Jessica exclaimed. "Lila will be so jealous that she didn't think of this first. Maybe Mom will even let me get a new dress for the occasion," she added happily.

"Before you start thinking about a new dress, we'd better ask Mom and Dad if we can have the party," Elizabeth said. "And I don't think we can ask *lots* of people. Our dining room table doesn't seat that many people."

"Whatever you say, Lizzie," Jessica said. "Come on, let's go ask them right now." Elizabeth grabbed her cookbook and followed her sister out the bedroom door.

They found their parents in the living room, reading the Sunday newspaper. Their fourteen-year-old brother, Steven, was there, too, stretched out on the floor with the Sports Section. Elizabeth knew he'd make a wisecrack or two when he heard their plans.

"Elizabeth and I have the best idea," Jessica began. "It's really fabulous."

Their parents looked up with curiosity.

"Well, don't keep us in suspense," Mrs. Wakefield said. "What is it?"

"We want to give a party," Elizabeth began, but then Jessica took over. "Not just an ordinary party. A dinner party! An elegant one, with a lace tablecloth, flowers, candlesticks, and French food."

"I want to make this recipe," Elizabeth said, showing her mother the picture in the cookbook. "And chocolate mousse, too, with real whipped cream."

At the mention of food, Steven looked up. "Hey, I like the sound of that."

"And we'll make everyone dress up for it," Jessica added. "The girls will wear long dresses and the boys will wear suits."

"You're not getting *me* into a suit!" Steven exclaimed.

"No problem," Jessica replied with a smile.

"You're not invited." She turned back to her parents. "We thought we'd have about fourteen kids from school."

Her mother's eyebrows shot up. "Fourteen? For a sit-down dinner?"

"Actually, we'd only be inviting twelve," Elizabeth said hastily. "It's fourteen including us."

"Isn't it a great idea?" Jessica asked eagerly.

Mr. and Mrs. Wakefield exchanged looks. "I'm sorry, girls," Mrs. Wakefield began slowly. "But I'm afraid I have to disagree. I think this is too big an undertaking for you. It's not really appropriate at your age. A dinner party like this takes a lot of work and a lot of planning."

"And a lot of money," added Mr. Wakefield. "How were you going to pay for all this fancy food?"

Elizabeth bit her lower lip. "Maybe it wouldn't cost so much," she offered.

Her mother shook her head. "When you're a little older you can start having dinner parties, girls." She noticed how disappointed the twins looked, and smiled gently. "But I've got another idea. Why don't you have a cookout for your friends? Your father just finished fencing in the backyard, and you could have a nice party out there. You could grill hot dogs and hamburgers."

"Oh, Mom," Jessica complained. "Everyone has cookouts. And hot dogs and hamburgers are so boring. Can't we have a dinner party, *please*? We want to do something special."

Elizabeth agreed with Jessica, but she could tell by the way her parents were shaking their heads that the fancy dinner party was out of the question.

"Maybe we could think of a way to make the cookout special," she whispered. Jessica shrugged her shoulders, and walked out of the room. Elizabeth followed close behind.

"Hey," Steven called after them, "you can still make that chocolate whatchamacallit for me!"

"Honestly!" Jessica wailed after they got back to Elizabeth's room. "I can't believe Mom and Dad are treating us like such babies!"

"If only there were something we could do to prove to them that we're responsible," Elizabeth said.

Jessica sighed slightly. "Forget it, Elizabeth. They're just not going to take us seriously. I'm so depressed! I was really getting excited about that party. Now there's nothing to look forward to."

"There's a four-day weekend coming up soon," Elizabeth announced, trying to sound cheerful. She went over to her desk and examined the calendar on the wall.

Jessica let out a sigh. "Big deal. Who cares about a long weekend when there's nothing special to do? I wish we could go somewhere."

Elizabeth was still studying the calendar. "You know, Great-Aunt Helen's birthday is right around that time."

"That's right." Jessica's expression turned into a small smile. "Great-Aunt Helen is so neat."

Elizabeth agreed. "Remember when we visited her last year? I love Sandy Harbor."

"Me, too," Jessica said. "Sandy Harbor has a great beach. And all the kids we met were so much fun."

"You mean the *boys*," Elizabeth teased. But she had also had a wonderful time. "Jess! Let's ask Mom and Dad if we can go visit Great-Aunt Helen over that long weekend!"

The gloom on Jessica's face lifted completely, and she sat up. "That's a fantastic idea, Lizzie." With that, the two girls ran back downstairs.

Luckily, Steven had disappeared. At least they'd be able to make their request without any wisecracks from him.

Mrs. Wakefield smiled knowingly at the sight of their cheerful faces. "I think we're about to hear another fabulous proposal," she said to her husband.

This time Elizabeth took charge. "We've got a

long weekend coming up in three weeks. We thought it would be fun to go visit Great-Aunt Helen."

"Oh, honey," Mrs. Wakefield said sympathetically. "I'm afraid that's impossible. Your father and I are both awfully busy at work, and we just can't get away."

"We didn't mean everyone. We meant just us," Jessica said. "Elizabeth and me—by ourselves."

"Alone?" Mr. Wakefield questioned. "All the way to Sandy Harbor? How would you get there?"

"There must be a bus," Elizabeth said. Her heart sank as she saw that her mother didn't look thrilled by the idea.

"I don't know, girls," Mrs. Wakefield said slowly. "Going to Sandy Harbor alone isn't like going to the Valley Mall. It's a long trip. I'm not sure you two are ready to travel that far by yourselves."

"Oh, Mom, please," Jessica urged. "We're not babies. We're old enough *and* grown up enough to take care of ourselves. Just give us a chance to prove it!"

Mr. Wakefield looked at them seriously. "Have you checked to find out how much the fare is?"

Elizabeth hadn't thought about that. "No . . ."

"I'll go find out right now," Jessica offered.

"I'll call the bus station." She disappeared into the kitchen, while Elizabeth sat down on the sofa next to her father. She couldn't understand why her father was so worried about money all of a sudden.

"Dad, can't you afford to send us to see Great-Aunt Helen?"

"That's not the point, Elizabeth. I'm simply concerned that you girls don't seem to understand the value of money. You probably haven't even considered the fact that trips cost money. And money doesn't grow on trees, you know."

"We're not accusing you and Jessica of being irresponsible," Mrs. Wakefield said. "But you come up with ideas without thinking them through. You have to stop to consider what they involve."

Before Elizabeth could reply, Jessica came bounding back into the room. "It's only twenty dollars," she announced.

Mrs. Wakefield looked surprised. "Twenty dollars round-trip?"

"I don't know," Jessica said. "I just asked how much it costs to go to Sandy Harbor from Sweet Valley."

"Then a round-trip ticket would be forty dollars," Mr. Wakefield informed her. "And don't forget there are two of you, so that brings the total to eighty dollars."

"Wow! That's a lot of money," Jessica exclaimed.

"Yes, Jessica, you're right," Mr. Wakefield confirmed. "It *is* a lot of money."

The twins exchanged looks. "Does that mean we can't go?" they asked at the same time.

Their parents were silent for a minute. "What do you think, Ned?" Mrs. Wakefield asked.

"I think," Mr. Wakefield said slowly, "that if they can prove they're responsible, they can go to Sandy Harbor."

Jessica clapped her hands in glee, but Elizabeth gazed at her father questioningly. "How can we prove we're responsible?"

Her father smiled. "By earning your own money for the fare."

Jessica's smile faded. "How?" she asked, bewildered.

"That's for you two to figure out," Mr. Wakefield replied.

Elizabeth nodded. "We can do that. Thanks, Dad, Mom." She got up and turned to her sister. "C'mon, Jess. We've got some thinking to do."

Two

◇

"Eighty dollars," Elizabeth mused as the girls settled back on her bed. "And we've got less than three weeks to earn it. We'd better come up with a good idea fast."

"Maybe we could sell something," Jessica suggested. Her eyes roamed Elizabeth's room, and settled on her bookshelves. "Like your books. You've got so many. Maybe they're worth eighty dollars."

"No way! I object!" Elizabeth was not about to part with her books. "How about selling your bracelet?" she countered.

Jessica clasped her hand over her silver bracelet as if Elizabeth had threatened to snatch it away. "Are you kidding? It's my favorite! Why don't we just make something we can sell?"

"Like what?"

Jessica's eyes lit up. "Hey, remember that orange cake you made last week? It was great! Maybe you could make four of them, and we could sell them for twenty dollars each."

"That's not a bad idea," Elizabeth said thoughtfully.

Just then, their mother appeared at the door. "Have you two come up with any more brilliant ideas?" she asked, smiling.

"How does this sound?" Elizabeth asked her. "I could make four orange cakes, and sell them for twenty dollars each."

"That was *my* idea," Jessica announced proudly.

"And it's not a bad one," Mrs. Wakefield replied. "But there's one problem. The bakery sells the same cakes for about ten dollars. Do you think people would be willing to pay twice the price for Elizabeth's?"

"I could bake eight cakes, then," Elizabeth said.

"But don't forget," her mother continued, "there are expenses involved. You have to buy all the ingredients to make the cakes. That would run into some money, too."

Elizabeth thought about what that meant. "So we'd only make a small profit for each cake." She did some quick division in her head. "I'd have to make about sixteen cakes!" She turned to her sister. "We'd better come up with another idea."

"Good luck, girls," Mrs. Wakefield said lightly, as she left the room.

Elizabeth frowned. "Maybe we should think about *doing* something for money, instead of *making* something—providing some kind of service, or something. Ken Matthews mows lawns to earn money." Ken was also in the sixth grade at Sweet Valley Middle School. He and Elizabeth were good friends.

"I don't want to mow lawns!" Jessica exclaimed.

"I know someone who has a newspaper route," Elizabeth offered.

Jessica wrinkled her nose. "That's an awful job. You have to get up really early in the morning. And what if it rains, like today?"

Elizabeth glanced out the window. "It looks like the rain's stopped." The clouds had disappeared, the sun was out, and she could see a couple of people walking dogs down the street. Suddenly, she had an inspiration.

"I've got it! I know what we can do to earn the money!"

"What?"

"We can start a dog-walking service!"

Jessica's mouth fell open. "We're going to walk dogs?"

"Sure," Elizabeth said with enthusiasm. "I'm sure a lot of dog owners would rather be doing other things. I'll bet they'd pay us to walk their dogs for them!"

Jessica made a face. "You know I don't like dogs. Mrs. Bramble's cocker spaniel was enough for me," she said, referring to a dog-sitting job she had once taken.

"Oh, come on, Jess. It'll only be for a couple of weeks," Elizabeth said. "Do you have any better ideas?"

"No," Jessica replied dejectedly. "How much can we charge?"

"Let's figure it out." Elizabeth got a notepad and a pencil from her desk. "OK, we need eighty dollars. If we each walk two dogs a day every day for the next two weeks—"

"Wait a minute," Jessica interrupted. "Not on

the weekends! I absolutely refuse to do this on weekends."

"OK, just after school, then. That makes ten days, times four dogs per day. If we charge two dollars a dog, we'll have exactly eighty dollars."

Jessica still wasn't enthusiastic. "Why dogs?" she groaned. "There must be a better way."

"Jess, this is a great idea!" Elizabeth said excitedly. "We just have to make flyers offering our services. I'll make one right now, and tomorrow we can photocopy it at school. Then in the afternoon we can hand them out to people walking dogs."

"I'm supposed to go to a Unicorn meeting after school tomorrow," Jessica objected.

"Well, you'll just have to skip it this time," Elizabeth said impatiently. "Look, Jess, do you want to go to Sandy Harbor or not?"

Jessica let out a deep sigh and nodded.

Elizabeth went to her desk and took out a marking pen and a sheet of paper. After a moment, she carefully printed: DOG-WALKING SERVICE. $2.00 PER DAY. CALL ELIZABETH OR JESSICA WAKEFIELD. She added their phone number, and then she paused.

"We're going to need money for the photocopying machine," she said. "I've got two dollars. How much do you have?"

"About a dollar," Jessica said. "How much will it cost?"

Elizabeth thought. "It's twenty cents a copy." She did some calculations on a piece of paper. "Uh-oh. We'll only be able to photocopy fifteen flyers. That's not enough. We need at least forty."

"Maybe we can borrow some money from Mom and Dad," Jessica suggested.

Elizabeth shook her head. "No, we want to show them we can handle this on our own. Let's see if Steven will lend us five dollars."

They found their brother outside in the driveway, dribbling a basketball. "Let me take care of this," Jessica whispered to Elizabeth. "I know how to handle him." She ambled over to Steven and smiled sweetly.

"I was just thinking of making some chocolate chip cookies," she said. "Want me to make extra so you can take some to school tomorrow?"

Steven looked at her suspiciously. "What do you want this time, Jessica?"

"Why, Steven," Jessica said innocently. "What makes you think I want anything?"

"Because your name is Jessica Wakefield."

"Steven!" Jessica wailed.

He grinned. "See, I knew you wanted something."

Elizabeth jumped in and quickly explained the dog-walking service, and why they needed to borrow five dollars.

"Five dollars, hmmm. How much interest are you willing to pay?"

Elizabeth looked at her brother in disbelief. "You're going to charge us interest?"

"Of course," Steven said. "You have to pay me back a little extra in exchange for the loan."

"How much is a little extra?" Jessica asked.

"Let me think." Steven scratched his head. "Fifty percent sounds good to me."

"Fifty percent!" Elizabeth didn't know much about interest, but fifty percent sounded outrageous. "That means we'd have to pay back seven dollars and fifty cents!"

"Take it or leave it," Steven said with a smug grin.

Elizabeth threw her hands up. "We don't have any choice." She turned to her sister. "This means we have to earn eighty-seven dollars and fifty cents."

"That's a *lot* of dogs," Jessica cried.

"Oh, and girls," Steven called as they headed

toward the house, "don't forget my chocolate chip cookies."

The next morning, before homeroom, the twins headed directly to the library to photocopy the flyer.

"Oh, no. There's Lila," Jessica gasped. "Quick, hide the flyer."

Elizabeth obediently stuck the piece of paper in her notebook, but she looked at her sister curiously. "Why, do we have to keep this a secret?"

"I just don't want Lila to know I have to *work* to get money," Jessica hissed.

Lila Fowler came from one of the wealthiest families in Sweet Valley. She would never even think of getting a job to earn money, Elizabeth thought as she watched Jessica's friend approach them.

Lila barely acknowledged Elizabeth as she addressed Jessica. "We're having the Unicorn meeting at my cousin Janet's house this afternoon."

Jessica looked miserable. Janet Howell was the president of the Unicorns, and she was an eighth grader. She would probably be angry if Jessica missed the meeting. But she had no choice. "I can't come. Elizabeth and I have some things to do."

Lila raised her eyebrows. "What could possibly be more important than a Unicorn meeting?"

Jessica looked at Elizabeth in desperation. "We've got errands to run," Elizabeth stated. "Family stuff."

Lila simply tossed her shoulder-length brown hair and fixed stern eyes on Jessica. "Then you'd better come with me now to tell Janet you won't be there."

Jessica gave Elizabeth another pleading look, and Elizabeth nodded reluctantly. She could handle the photocopying by herself. "Go ahead. But don't forget to meet me right after school," she said firmly.

"I won't," Jessica promised, and she ran off with Lila. Elizabeth went into the library, stopping at the main desk to get change for the copy machine. Then she went over to the copier and carefully aligned the flyer on the screen.

"Hi, Elizabeth. What are you doing?"

Elizabeth turned and smiled at Ken Matthews. "Jessica and I are trying to earn enough money to go on a trip. So we're starting a dog-walking business." She showed him the flyer.

"Neat!" Ken exclaimed. "Gee, I love dogs."

"Really? Then why don't you have one?"

Ken's smile faded, and he shook his head

sadly. "Every time I ask my parents if I can have a dog, they say no."

"Why?"

"They think I'm not old enough to be responsible for a dog. They won't even give me a chance to prove that I am."

Elizabeth nodded sympathetically. "I know what you mean. My parents don't think Jessica and I are very responsible either."

Ken leaned against the machine, folded his arms, and frowned. "Sometimes I think adults just don't take us very seriously. But listen, if you need any help with your dog-walking, let me know, OK?"

"Sure," Elizabeth said. "I think we'll get a lot of customers."

"Great," Ken replied. "I'll see you later."

Elizabeth concentrated on her photocopying, checking each copy to make sure it was perfect. The flyer looked pretty professional to her, and she felt sure it would impress people. As the copies came out of the machine, she began to feel more and more optimistic. Dog owners would jump at the chance to have their pets walked for them. And once Jessica saw how easy it was to earn money, she wouldn't object any more.

"Sandy Harbor, here we come," Elizabeth

said to herself as she gathered her flyers and hurried off to homeroom.

After school that afternoon, Elizabeth stood in front of the school entrance, tapping her foot impatiently. As usual, Jessica was late.

"C'mon, Jess!" Elizabeth yelled when she finally spotted her sister.

"I'm coming," Jessica grumbled. "Couldn't you hand these flyers out by yourself? I really need to go to that Unicorn meeting."

"No," Elizabeth replied flatly. "We're in this together, Jess. Now stop complaining."

They had only walked one block from school when they spotted their first dog. It was a sweet-looking poodle, trotting beside an elderly woman.

"Excuse me," Elizabeth said to the woman. She held out a flyer. "We're starting a dog-walking service. Would you be interested?"

The woman smiled, but shook her head. "No, thank you, dears. Walking Fifi is the only exercise I get."

"Oh. Well, in case you change your mind, won't you take one?" The woman accepted it, and walked on.

"That was stupid," Jessica said. "That flyer

cost twenty cents. And that woman's not even going to call us."

"Well, you never know," Elizabeth replied. "Look, there's another dog." She hurried down the street, while Jessica trailed after her.

"I don't like the looks of that one," Jessica said. "He's too big."

"We can't afford to be choosy, Jess." The large Labrador was tugging at the leash held by a young man.

"Hello," Elizabeth said to the man. "Would you be interested in having your dog walked?" She handed him a flyer.

The man looked at her doubtfully. "I don't think either of you girls could handle Buster. Or both of you together, for that matter. He gets pretty feisty."

"We're stronger than we look, and . . ." Elizabeth started to say.

"But not that strong," Jessica interrupted to agree with the man. "C'mon, Lizzie." She grabbed her sister's arm and pulled her away.

"What did you say that for?" Elizabeth demanded. "I think I could have talked him into it."

"I don't want to get near that dog," Jessica replied. "He looked mean. We have to find small, quiet dogs."

The girls walked up and down the streets, looking for small dogs, but there didn't seem to be many out that day. After two hours of walking, they'd only given out five flyers.

"My feet hurt," Jessica whined. "And I'm tired."

"So am I, but we've still got a bunch of flyers left."

"Oh, come on, Elizabeth. It'll take us hours to find that many dogs," Jessica complained. "And I'm hungry. If we don't start home, we'll be late for supper." She paused. "And then Mom and Dad will really think we're irresponsible."

"You're right," Elizabeth said. "But why don't we stick the rest of these flyers on cars parked along the road?"

"How do you know if the car owners have dogs?" Jessica asked.

"We don't," Elizabeth replied. "But we have to take a chance."

By the time the twins got home, they were completely exhausted.

"All that work, and we haven't earned any money yet," Jessica commented as they walked into the house.

"Let's just keep our fingers crossed," Elizabeth said, trying to feel optimistic. "Who knows?

Maybe every single one of those car owners has a dog."

Jessica didn't seem optimistic at all. "Maybe. But I just hope they're all little quiet ones."

The family was just sitting down to dinner when the phone rang. Mr. Wakefield got up to answer it.

"Hello?" He listened, then turned to the others. "A Mrs. Foster calling for either Elizabeth or Jessica."

"I'll take it," Elizabeth said. Her father handed her the phone.

"Hello, this is Elizabeth Wakefield."

"I found your flyer on my car," the voice on the other end said. "I was wondering if you'd walk my dog on Tuesday and Thursday."

"We'd be happy to," Elizabeth said. She picked up the notepad and pencil lying beside the phone. "Just give me your address and we'll come by for the dog. Is three-thirty OK?"

"Fine," the woman said, and then gave Elizabeth her address.

No sooner had Elizabeth hung up the phone when it rang again.

"Hello?" she answered excitedly.

"Is this one of the girls I met when I was

walking my dog this afternoon?'' It sounded like the man with the big Labrador.

''Yes, this is Elizabeth Wakefield.''

''Well, I happen to be very busy this week, so if you girls really think you can handle Buster, I'll use your services.''

''Great!'' Elizabeth exclaimed. She picked up the pad and pencil again. ''What days would you like your dog walked?''

''Tuesday through Friday,'' the man said. Elizabeth wrote down the man's address, gave him a time when she would come by, and thanked him.

''Our first customers!'' she cried out gleefully when she hung up. ''See, Jess, I told you this would work!''

''What's going on here?'' Mrs. Wakefield asked.

''Jessica and I are going to walk dogs to earn money for the Sandy Harbor trip,'' Elizabeth told her.

''Well!'' exclaimed Mr. Wakefield. ''I'm impressed! You girls *are* taking this seriously!''

''Did you ask them how big the dogs are?'' Jessica asked with concern.

''No.'' Elizabeth decided not to mention the large Labrador. There was no need to make Jessica nervous ahead of time.

Just then, the phone rang again. This time it was a woman with two dogs who needed the girls on Wednesday and Friday afternoon.

"This is fantastic!" Elizabeth said as she sat down at the table. "We might even make more money than we need for the trip."

Jessica brightened. "Gee, maybe I could even get that new outfit I saw last week at the mall."

"I hope you don't mind if the phones are ringing all evening," Elizabeth told her parents proudly.

"If business really starts booming, you girls might have to get your own phone." Mr. Wakefield beamed.

But Elizabeth had spoken too soon. The phone didn't ring again all evening. By nine o'clock, her earlier elation had disappeared.

She sat down at her desk and did some figuring. Two dogs on Tuesday, three on Wednesday, two on Thursday, three on Friday. At two dollars a dog, that made twenty dollars.

She went to Jessica's room and showed her. "It's a start," she said. "But it's not much for a week's work, especially since we've only got three weeks before the long weekend."

Jessica stared at the figures in dismay. "We need sixty dollars more."

"Sixty-seven fifty," Elizabeth reminded her. "Don't forget the money we borrowed from Steven."

"I know *he* won't forget," Jessica noted.

Elizabeth agreed. She tried to think positively, but it wasn't easy. They were a long way from meeting their goal. If they were really going to make it to Sandy Harbor, they were going to have to find a lot more dogs that needed walking.

Three

◈

At three-thirty on Tuesday afternoon, Elizabeth and Jessica arrived at the home of their first client. Jessica waited at the bottom of the steps, her arms folded and her expression grim. Elizabeth rang the bell, and a woman opened the door almost immediately.

"You must be the Wakefield girls," she said. "My goodness! You're identical twins!"

They'd heard this many times before, but Elizabeth smiled and nodded politely, enjoying the expression on the woman's face.

"Wait right here," the woman said, "and I'll get Bitsy." She disappeared for a moment, and came back with a small cocker spaniel. Elizabeth noted the relief that crossed Jessica's face. She knew she'd be seeing a completely different expression when Jessica saw the dog they were picking up next.

"We'll have Bitsy back in one hour," Elizabeth said, taking the dog from the woman who then closed the door. Elizabeth set the spaniel on the ground and handed the leash to Jessica.

"Why do *I* have to hold on to him?" Jessica asked peevishly.

"It's a *she*," Elizabeth told her. "We're getting the next dog right down the block and I'll be walking him."

When Jessica recognized the man who answered the door at the next house, she gasped. And when Buster emerged from behind him, leapt up, and began licking Jessica's face, she shrieked.

"He likes you!" the man said with delight. "Don't worry, he won't hurt you. He gets pretty lively, but he's a very friendly dog."

"I can see that," Elizabeth said, laughing as Buster proceeded to give her the same treatment he'd given Jessica.

Jessica, practically in tears, was not quite as amused by Buster's behavior. "He licked me!" she wailed as they left the doorstep. "He touched my face with his slobbery tongue!"

"Oh, Jess, don't be such a baby," Elizabeth said. "He didn't hurt you."

"Well, maybe not, but it felt disgusting. And he'd better not try it again."

"Don't worry," Elizabeth reassured her. "I'll walk Buster."

The Labrador was eager to explore and Elizabeth had to trot to keep up with him. As she concentrated on keeping a firm grip on Buster's leash, Jessica strolled along behind her with her well-behaved cocker spaniel.

Then, out of the corner of her eye, Elizabeth saw something whiz past her. With a start, she realized it was Bitsy. Still gripping Buster's leash, she twisted her head to see what had happened. To her amazement, she saw Jessica calmly gathering her hair into a ponytail.

"Jess!" she yelled. "What are you doing?"

"My hair was getting in my eyes," Jessica replied. She glanced around casually. "Where's Bitsy? I told her to stay."

"Well, she didn't! Go get her!"

Luckily, Bitsy hadn't gone too far. She was sniffing intently around the base of a tree. Jessica gazed at the cocker spaniel with distaste. Slowly, she dragged herself over to the tree, and gingerly took hold of Bitsy's leash.

"This is a real drag," she fumed.

"Cheer up," Elizabeth urged. Buster then tugged on his leash and dragged Elizabeth halfway down the street before she could say anything more.

On Wednesday, they picked up Buster first. Elizabeth was starting to get used to his frisky pulling and tugging, but she still had to concentrate all of her energy on showing him who was in control. As they approached the house of their next client, a lady greeted them at the door with a Yorkshire terrier in each arm.

"You're going to have to take both of them," Elizabeth told Jessica.

Jessica went pale. "*Both* of them? I have to walk two dogs at the same time?"

"You've got two free hands," Elizabeth argued. "It takes both of mine to handle Buster."

Jessica groaned for the hundredth time that week.

"You know, I could be at Lila's house right now, having a great time. She invited all the Unicorns to go swimming."

Elizabeth was getting tired of Jessica's constant complaining. The two terriers were exactly the kind of dog Jessica could handle—small and undemanding. And here she was acting as if they were two gigantic wolfhounds.

Elizabeth tried to think of some way to distract her sister. "Let's walk the dogs downtown," she suggested. "Then we can window-shop while we're walking."

Jessica brightened for a second, then frowned. "What if I run into someone I know?"

"You just told me they're all at Lila's."

"Oh, right. I guess it's OK, then."

Looking in the store windows did manage to keep Jessica from moaning and groaning. "Oooh, Lizzie, look at that gorgeous jumpsuit!" she cried out.

Elizabeth pulled on Buster's leash. "Stay," she ordered him. To her surprise, the dog obeyed, and Elizabeth looked in the store window.

"That *is* pretty," she said, admiring the outfit.

"I wonder if it comes in purple," Jessica murmured. "Oh, Lizzie, I've just got to try it on."

"I don't think they'll let us bring dogs in the store," Elizabeth noted.

"Couldn't you hold them all out here while I go in and try it on?" Jessica asked. "It'll only take a minute."

Elizabeth frowned. Buster was acting pretty calm, but holding on to three dogs at the same time was going to be very difficult.

"Please?" Jessica pleaded.

Elizabeth knew if she said no, Jessica would start whining again. "All right," she relented. "But make it fast, OK?"

"You're the best!" Jessica told her sister. She handed her two leashes and ran inside the store.

When Jessica's 'minute' turned into twenty minutes, Elizabeth began to lose her patience. The terriers, in turn, began yelping.

Then all three dogs decided to move in opposite directions. Elizabeth pulled and yanked the leashes while yelling for Jessica to come out. Buster finished by hauling Elizabeth down the street while the two terriers, unable to keep up, howled pitifully as they were dragged along.

Panting and sweating, Elizabeth finally got Buster to turn around. She led the dogs back to the boutique just as Jessica was coming out.

Elizabeth glared at her. "You said you were only going to be a minute!"

"Honestly, Lizzie, don't make such a fuss," Jessica said breezily. She took the terriers' leashes and glanced at her watch. "Oh, good. It's time to take them back. Gee, the time flew by quickly today."

"How's the dog-walking coming along?" Amy

Sutton asked Elizabeth as they walked out of class Thursday afternoon.

Elizabeth had barely seen her best friend that week.

"Not so great," Elizabeth confessed. "We don't have enough money yet for our trip. And Jessica's always complaining and goofing off."

"I wish I could help you out," Amy said sympathetically. "But I've got Booster practice this afternoon, and I'm babysitting after school. Do you have to walk the dogs on Saturday?"

"No, thank goodness," Elizabeth replied.

"Great. Julie, Nora, and I are going roller skating at the rink," Amy told her. "Can you come?"

"I'd love to," Elizabeth said gratefully. After a week of dog-walking, she knew she deserved a day of fun. "That sounds wonderful." She glanced up at the clock on the wall. "I'd better go meet Jessica. I'll see you later."

As she headed toward the hall exit, she wondered why she was bothering to hurry. She was pleased, however, to find Jessica already there, waiting for her. Maybe Jessica was finally learning the meaning of responsibility, Elizabeth thought happily.

But as she got closer, she noticed that Jessica's eyes were just a little too bright, and her smile just a little too big. Jessica was up to something.

"Elizabeth, how many dogs do we have to walk today?"

"Two," Elizabeth replied. "Buster and Bitsy. Why?"

Jessica bit her lower lip, and cocked her head to one side. "The Boosters are having a practice this afternoon. And I just *have* to go. We're learning some new cheers. If I miss this practice, I'll be so far behind . . ."

The Boosters were Sweet Valley Middle School's cheering squad. Elizabeth recalled Amy having mentioned practice, too. Still, they had committed themselves to walking the dogs.

"But what about our dog-walking? That's important, too."

"I know." Jessica nodded solemnly. "But if you could just handle the dogs by yourself today, I promise I'll make it up to you."

"How?"

"I don't know. But I'll think of something, I promise," Jessica assured her.

Elizabeth sighed. She didn't really want to let Jessica off the hook, but she knew how important the Boosters were to her. And she *could* handle Buster and Bitsy by herself.

"All right," she said finally. "But just this once."

"Thanks, Lizzie! You're the greatest sister in the whole world!" Jessica ran back into the building as Elizabeth went off alone to gather the dogs.

The next afternoon, Elizabeth stood in front of the school entrance, her arms folded and her lips pressed together in annoyance. Jessica was fifteen minutes late.

"Hi, Elizabeth." Ken Matthews paused on the school steps. "What are you doing?"

"Waiting for Jessica," Elizabeth told him. "We have to go pick up our dogs."

Ken looked puzzled. "I just saw Jessica. She was with a bunch of kids and they were headed for Casey's Place."

"Casey's Place!" Elizabeth's mouth fell open. She couldn't believe what she'd just heard. "Jessica can't go to an ice cream parlor! We've got a job!"

"Maybe she forgot," Ken suggested.

Sure, Elizabeth thought grimly. *Jessica forgot, all right—on purpose.* She was tempted to storm into the ice cream parlor and embarrass Jessica in front of all her friends.

Suddenly Elizabeth remembered something, and clapped a hand to her mouth.

"Oh, no," she moaned. "We've got three dogs

to walk this afternoon. How am I going to handle them by myself?"

"I'll help you," Ken offered. "I'm not doing anything this afternoon."

Elizabeth looked at him gratefully. "Oh, Ken, would you? I'll give you half of what I'm paid."

"I don't want any money, Elizabeth," Ken said, shaking his head. "I love being around dogs. I'll do it just for fun."

Elizabeth grinned. "OK, but don't call it fun yet. Not until you've met Buster!"

With Ken, walking the dogs was a lot more fun than it had been with Jessica. He played with Buster, and the big Labrador trotted along happily by his side. The terriers even wagged their tails and let out a few barks of contentment.

"You should have a dog of your own," Elizabeth told him.

"I know," Ken said, sighing. "I just wish I could convince my parents of that."

Elizabeth understood. "Parents are like that, I guess. I know mine don't think Jessica and I are very responsible either. They don't think we can actually raise the money to go to Great-Aunt Helen's by ourselves."

"Have you saved enough money for the trip yet?"

"No. And I don't know how we're going to get enough. Jessica hates dog-walking, and I can't walk enough dogs to earn the money by myself. With a little luck, we'll think of something else."

Sure enough, luck was on her side that day. After returning Buster, they went to drop the terriers off. "I'm going out of town tomorrow," their owner told Elizabeth. "Would you be able to keep the dogs at your home Saturday and Sunday?"

"Well," Elizabeth hesitated. "I don't know. I'll have to ask my parents."

"I can pay you twenty dollars," the woman said. "All you'd have to do is feed them and walk them. Actually, they could use a bath, too."

"It doesn't sound like a problem. I'll call and let you know tonight," Elizabeth told the woman. As soon as the door closed, she turned to Ken excitedly. "Twenty dollars! That would put us halfway to our goal!"

But when Elizabeth brought up dog-sitting to her parents, neither of them looked pleased.

"That's a big job," her father said. "If anything happened to those terriers, you and Jessica would be responsible."

"Nothing will happen to them. We'll keep them in the backyard, and we'll make sure the fence gate is kept closed."

"But where will they sleep?" Mrs. Wakefield asked. "I don't want dogs in the house."

"They won't have to come into the house at all. They can sleep on old blankets in Dad's tool-shed," Elizabeth said. "We can even bathe them out back with the garden hose."

"It sounds like you've got all this figured out," Mrs. Wakefield said. "What does Jessica think? Where is she, anyway?"

"Oh, she had something to do," Elizabeth said vaguely. She didn't want her parents to know Jessica had shirked her dog-walking responsibility. Otherwise, they'd never let them keep the dogs over the weekend.

"We'll take turns watching them," she assured her parents. "Honest, we can handle it."

After exchanging looks with his wife, Mr. Wakefield finally nodded. "All right, you can dog-sit. But remember, this is your responsibility. I don't want to hear any complaints if those dogs give you problems. You two are on your own."

"I know," Elizabeth replied. "And thanks!" She ran upstairs to call the terriers' owner.

Just as Elizabeth hung up the phone, she saw Jessica coming up the stairs. She folded her arms and glared at her sister.

"Gee, Lizzie, I'm sorry," Jessica said, her voice

dripping with honey. "When Lila asked me to go to Casey's I got a craving for ice cream and I completely forgot about the dogs!"

"That's OK, Jess," Elizabeth said in a voice almost as sweet as her sister's. "You can make it up to me this weekend. We're going to get twenty dollars for keeping those terriers over the weekend. Isn't that great? Then we'll have half of what we need to get to Sandy Harbor."

"Hooray!" Jessica exclaimed.

"But you have to promise me you'll be home tomorrow," Elizabeth continued. "The dogs have to be watched and bathed and fed. Do you absolutely, positively promise me that you'll be here?"

"I promise," Jessica said solemnly.

"Good." Elizabeth grinned. "Because tomorrow *I'm* going roller skating."

She got a brief but satisfying glimpse of her sister's shocked face before whirling around and going to her room.

Four
◇

Jessica sat on the back steps with her chin in her hands. The terriers had been dropped off early that morning and were now frolicking in the yard. Jessica watched them with dread. She didn't like the idea of spending the entire day alone with them.

Elizabeth had already left to meet her friends at the skating rink. "Remember to feed them and to keep the gate closed," she had instructed Jessica. "And don't forget to bathe them. I left some old towels in the kitchen for you to use."

Jessica was about to protest when Elizabeth reminded her, "You owe me this, Jess. You haven't done your share this week, and you know it. So if you want to go to Sandy Harbor, this is your chance to make up for everything you didn't do."

Now Jessica cringed as one of the terriers came toward her and nipped at her feet. Then the other one joined him, and both of them started yelping and jumping up.

"I'm *not* going to play with you," Jessica snapped at them. "I'll watch you, but that's it."

The dogs didn't go away, however. In fact, their yelps soon turned into howls.

"Maybe you're hungry," Jessica said. "I'll get your food."

She got up and dragged herself into the kitchen. The woman who owned the terriers had left special food for them. But when Jessica opened the can she pushed it away from her. The contents smelled even more disgusting than it looked.

Gingerly, she spooned the dog food into a bowl. Holding it out at arm's length, she went back outside and placed it in front of the terriers.

She had been right—they were definitely hungry. Absently, she watched them bury their heads in the bowl, but in only a few minutes, they were back at her side, begging for attention. Jessica picked up a little rubber ball and threw it. The terriers ran after it, and one of them picked it up in his mouth. He ran back toward Jessica and dropped the ball at her feet.

Not wanting to touch the ball, she kicked it, and the dogs went after it.

What a way to spend a Saturday, Jessica thought mournfully.

"Jessica! What are you doing?"

She looked up and saw Lila Fowler and Ellen Riteman at the gate. *Oh, no*, she thought. How was she going to explain this?

"Hi," Jessica greeted them reluctantly. "I'm, uh, watching some neighbor's dogs for a while. What are you guys up to?"

"We're going to the mall," Lila told her. "Want to come?"

There was nothing Jessica liked more than spending a Saturday roaming around the Valley Mall with her friends. "I can't," she said regretfully. "I have to stay here with these dogs."

Lila gazed at her in amazement. "You mean, you're stuck here all day? Can't Elizabeth watch them for you?"

Jessica shook her head woefully. "She went roller skating and left me with this rotten job."

Lila sniffed. "Well, if I were you, I'd just leave. After all, the dogs won't go anywhere— they're fenced in."

"I can't leave them alone," Jessica murmured. She knew that Elizabeth would find out and that she'd tell their parents. Then she could just forget about going to Sandy Harbor.

At that moment, Ken Matthews rode up the walk on his bike, and hopped off. "Hi, everyone. Where's Elizabeth?"

"Having fun," Jessica grumbled, "while I'm stuck here with these dogs." She turned to her friends. "You guys want to stay here and help me take care of them?"

Ellen eyed the terriers and shuddered. "No thanks."

"C'mon, Ellen," Lila said. "I want to go shopping." She glanced at Jessica disdainfully. "Personally, I think you're crazy to stick around here when you could be with us at the mall."

Jessica watched forlornly as the two girls started to walk off. "Look, Jessica," Ken said, "if you want to go to the mall with your friends, I'll watch the dogs for you."

Jessica couldn't believe her ears. "You will? Would you give them a bath, too?"

"Sure, I'd be glad to." Ken opened the gate to let himself in. One of the terriers came bounding over and Ken scooped him up. "Hiya, fella," he said, letting the dog lick his face.

Jessica wrinkled her nose, but she was too excited to be disgusted. *Surely Elizabeth wouldn't mind as long as someone is watching the dogs*, she thought to herself. "Thanks, Ken! You're terrific!"

But Ken wasn't listening. He was sitting on the ground, looking positively blissful as the two terriers leapt all over him.

As Elizabeth came around to the backyard, she heard dogs barking and saw a ball go flying through the air. She was not only surprised but delighted that Jessica was being so attentive. It wasn't until she actually entered the back yard that she discovered it wasn't her sister at all.

"Hi, Ken. What are you doing here?"

"I just dropped by to see how you were getting along with the dogs." One of the terriers had returned with the ball. Ken took it from his mouth and threw it again. "These guys are terrific. They don't fight or anything. I've been having a great time playing with them."

Elizabeth noticed that the front of Ken's T-shirt was wet. "I can see you helped with the baths, too. I'll bet Jessica appreciated that." She looked around. "Where is she anyway?"

"She went to the mall with Lila and Ellen."

"Oh, no!" Elizabeth clenched her fists. "She's

impossible! She promised me she'd stay home with the dogs. I can't believe she just ran off and left them!"

Ken turned a little red. "Well, I told her she could. I mean, I could see she didn't want to be here with them. And I didn't have anything special to do. The dogs were never alone."

"That's not the point," Elizabeth stated. "I appreciate your staying with them. But it was her responsibility, and she should have been here." The more she thought about it, the angrier she grew. "Jessica doesn't deserve to go on that trip. I've just about had it with her. She's the most unreliable, selfish—"

"Whoa!" Ken interrupted. "Don't waste your lecture on me!"

Elizabeth couldn't help smiling. "Sorry. I'm just so furious. Jessica thinks she can get away with everything. I guess it's partly my fault, too, because I cover up for her. Well, this time, I won't. I'm going to let her know exactly what I think. And I can't wait!"

"You won't have to," Ken said. "Here she comes now."

Elizabeth turned and saw Jessica strolling up the walk, looking like she didn't have a care in the world.

"Hi," Jessica said breezily as she came through the gate. "How are the dogs?"

"I'm surprised you even care," Elizabeth snapped at her.

Jessica seemed taken aback by her tone. "What's the matter?"

"Jessica Wakefield, you promised you'd stay home today and take care of these dogs! And you just took off and left them!"

"I didn't leave them *alone*," Jessica objected. "Ken was here. And he *wanted* to stay with them. I didn't even ask him to. He offered."

"That's true," Ken admitted.

"It doesn't matter," Elizabeth said hotly. "It was your responsibility."

Jessica put her hands on her hips and faced her squarely. "Elizabeth, don't make such a big deal out of it."

"It *is* a big deal," Elizabeth insisted. "You're being inconsiderate and—"

She didn't get to continue with her list of adjectives. Suddenly Ken let out a long whistle. "Wow, get a load of that car!"

Elizabeth looked out at the road. A black sports car had pulled up in the driveway.

"Are Mom and Dad expecting someone?" Jessica asked.

"They're not even home," Elizabeth replied.

They all watched as a man emerged from the car. Then he pulled the front seat forward and snapped his fingers. A moment later, a beautiful white dog crept out.

"Who *is* that?" Jessica asked.

Elizabeth shook her head. "I don't know. I've never seen him before. I wonder what he wants."

"Well, it looks like we're about to find out," Ken said. Sure enough, the man and the dog were heading up the walk toward them.

Five

◇

There was something about the man's expression that made Elizabeth feel uncomfortable. His mouth was set in a thin line, and his pale blue eyes were cold and unfriendly.

She noticed that he was carrying one of the flyers she and Jessica had put on the cars. He glanced at it, and looked at the girls. "Are you Elizabeth and Jessica Wakefield?"

The twins nodded.

"My name is Quincy," the man said. "I need a place to leave my dog for a week while I'm out of town on business."

Elizabeth and Jessica looked at each other. "We'd have to ask our parents," Elizabeth said.

"Then go ask them," the man said bluntly.

"They're not home right now," Elizabeth told him. "But if you'll leave me your phone number, I'll ask them when they get home and then I'll call you."

"I can't wait for that," the man said. "I have to leave for the airport right now. Look, I'll give you twenty dollars now, and twenty more when I pick him up next Saturday."

"That's forty dollars!" Jessica whispered to her sister. "That means we'll have enough for our trip!"

The same thought had occurred to Elizabeth. And as much as this man gave her the creeps, there was Sandy Harbor to think of. It wasn't as if they'd have to spend any time around *him*—just his dog.

"I don't think Mom and Dad would mind," she told Jessica. "As long as we don't bother them with it."

"And we've done a good job with the terriers," Jessica added.

Elizabeth raised her eyebrows and looked at her meaningfully. But Jessica ignored her and spoke to the man. "We'll do it!"

The man pulled a wallet from his pocket, and handed her twenty dollars. "Did you bring his food?" Elizabeth asked.

"No," the man said. He handed her a few more bills. "Here, you can buy some." Then, without saying goodbye to his dog, or even patting him on the head, he turned abruptly and started back toward his car.

"Mr. Quincy!" Elizabeth called after him.

The man looked back. "What do you want?"

"What's the dog's name?"

"Joe." And with that, the man climbed back into his car and drove away.

All this time, the dog had been sitting quietly outside the fence, his head down. Elizabeth opened the gate, but the dog didn't move. "C'mon, Joe," she said gently. The dog looked up for a second, and then his head went down again. Slowly he made his way into the yard.

Jessica was gazing dreamily at the twenty-dollar bill in her hands when Elizabeth deftly grabbed it from her. "I'll put this away," she said. She wasn't about to let her sister loose in Sweet Valley with a twenty-dollar bill.

"We can write Great-Aunt Helen tonight and tell her we're coming," Jessica said excitedly. "When Mr. Quincy comes back, we'll have all the money we need."

"Not quite," Elizabeth corrected her. "We have to pay Steven seven dollars and fifty cents, remember?"

Jessica brushed that aside. "Maybe we can get out of paying him back."

"How?"

"Oh, I don't know. Maybe we can offer to make his bed every day for a month, or do the dishes when it's his turn, that sort of thing."

Elizabeth grimaced. "You say 'we,' Jess, but you mean *me*. And I'm going to tell you something right now. If we're going to take care of this dog for a week, you're going to do your share of the work."

Jessica's eyes widened. "Oh, I will, Lizzie. I promise."

"Where have I heard that before," Elizabeth muttered.

"Hey, you two, come here." Ken was squatting on the ground, gazing at the dog who was standing motionless several feet from him.

"What's the matter?" Elizabeth asked as they joined him.

"Watch this." Ken extended his hand as if to pat the dog on the head. The dog backed away.

"That's funny," Elizabeth said. "Dogs usually come running to you." She moved closer to Joe, and the dog cowered. "I've never seen a dog act like this. He's acting like he's scared of us." She clapped her hands lightly. "Joe? Come here, Joe!" But the dog just shrank back.

"There's something really sad about this dog," Ken told them.

Jessica bent down to look, and straightened up almost immediately. "Ick, he smells."

"That's because he's dirty," Elizabeth said, crouching down next to Ken. "It looks like he hasn't had a bath in a long time."

Ken examined his paws. "And his nails haven't been clipped, either." He shook his head in bewilderment. "You know, this looks like a purebred Siberian Samoyed. But he looks like some stray who's been living on the streets."

"He does look awfully skinny," Jessica declared.

"Maybe he hasn't been fed enough," Ken said.

"Let's feed him right now," Elizabeth suggested. She ran into the kitchen and spooned some of the terriers' dog food into a bowl. "Here, Joe," she coaxed as she brought it outside and laid it on the ground near the dog.

The dog looked puzzled. Then, slowly and cautiously, he approached the bowl and sniffed it. He looked up at the twins and Ken in seeming disbelief. Finally, he devoured the food.

"Gee, he must have been starving," Ken said, amazed.

Even Jessica was watching Joe with concern. "I'll get him some water."

When the dog seemed like he'd eaten and drunk enough, Ken suggested a bath. "That might make him feel better."

"It'll definitely make him smell better," Jessica added.

Joe eyed them warily as they set about arranging his bath. Jessica gathered the shampoo and the towels. Ken unraveled the garden hose. As he dragged the hose toward Joe, the dog suddenly started shaking.

"Ken, look!" Elizabeth cried out in alarm. There was real fear in Joe's eyes. And then he started whimpering.

"Maybe he just doesn't like baths," Jessica suggested.

Ken looked puzzled. "It's the hose. He's staring at it like he's afraid of it." He set the hose on the ground, and the dog seemed to calm down a little.

"Maybe we should use something else," Elizabeth said. She went into the kitchen and came back out with a bucketful of lukewarm water.

Ken put his arms tenderly around the dog. He was barely touching him, but the dog flinched. Carefully, Elizabeth poured water over Joe. Jessica added some shampoo. Then, very gently, Elizabeth began rubbing the shampoo into his fur. In spite of her light touch, the dog whimpered, as if in pain.

"What's the matter, Joe?" Elizabeth asked. "I can't possibly be hurting you."

Then Ken gasped. "Look," he said. He pushed back Joe's fur. Elizabeth saw something that made her clap her hand over her mouth. Jessica looked horrified.

There was a big, raw-looking cut on the animal's body. "No wonder he's crying. The shampoo must be stinging him terribly," Elizabeth exclaimed. Quickly, she poured some water on the cut to wash away the soap.

But the dog still whimpered, and Ken and the twins soon realized why. They found more cuts and bruises on his body.

"Poor dog!" Jessica said. "I wonder what happened to him?"

"Maybe he was in a fight," Elizabeth said. "What do you think, Ken?"

Ken didn't say anything. He just gazed at the dog with sorrowful eyes. "Poor Joe," he whispered. Then he hugged him, and for once the dog didn't pull away.

Elizabeth filled the bucket with more water, and washed off the rest of the shampoo. Now that he was clean, they could all see what a beautiful dog Joe was. His wet hair, whiter than snow, glistened in the sunlight and hid the bruises on his body. But they all knew those bruises were there. And they watched the dog in silence.

"What do you think could have done this to him?" Elizabeth asked Ken.

Ken stood up. His face was pale, and his fists were clenched. "Someone's been abusing this dog."

Elizabeth was shocked. "You mean—on purpose? Someone's been hitting him?"

Ken nodded. "Someone has deliberately hurt him. A dog doesn't get bruises and cuts all over his body by accident."

His voice was harsh. Elizabeth had never seen Ken look so angry.

"Why would anyone want to hurt a dog?" Jessica asked.

A dreadful thought occurred to Elizabeth. "Do you think it could have been Mr. Quincy?"

Ken spoke through tightened lips. "Who else?"

"I don't get it," Jessica said. "Why would anyone beat his own dog?"

"I don't know," Ken said bitterly. "But I wish that Mr. Quincy was here right now. I'd show him some abuse."

"People like that shouldn't be allowed to have dogs," Elizabeth said passionately. "There must be something we can do."

"Maybe we should tell Mom and Dad," Jessica said.

Elizabeth shook her head. "Remember what they said? No complaining, no whining. If we go to them, they'll say it's our problem and we should take care of it." She bent down. Very, very gently, she patted Joe on the head. The dog cringed a little, but he didn't pull away as much as before.

"He's probably scared of people," she said. "He must think everyone is like Mr. Quincy."

Jessica knelt down beside the dog. "We won't hurt you, Joe. We're going to take good care of you."

"I want to help you take care of him," Ken said. "All this week, OK? I can come over after school."

Jessica and Elizabeth agreed.

"Maybe if we show him a lot of love, he won't be so scared of us," Ken said. Lightly, he stroked the dog's back. "Joe needs all the love we can give him."

Six

◇

"What's in the bag?" Elizabeth asked Ken as they walked home after school Monday.

Ken clutched the brown sack and grinned happily. "Just a few things for Joe I picked up. How was he this morning?"

"It's hard to say," Elizabeth replied. "I think he looked a little sad when I left. I just hope he wasn't lonely. The lady who owned the terriers took them back last night, so he was all alone in the yard today."

"Well, he's probably used to being alone," Ken noted as they turned up the walk toward the Wakefields' backyard. "I have a feeling that Mr.

Quincy doesn't spend a whole lot of time playing with him."

Joe was sitting quietly in the sun. When Ken and Elizabeth came in through the gate, he got up. He didn't run over to greet them, but he didn't back away either. Elizabeth could have sworn he looked happy to see them.

"Wait till you see what I got for you, buddy," Ken told the dog. Joe eyed the brown bag warily as Ken opened it. First, Ken pulled out a few dog toys—a rubber bone, a soft ball, and a plastic ring with bells that jingled. Joe sniffed at them tentatively. Then Ken took a large, soft brush for Joe's hair out of the sack, and a bag of dog food. "This is the best stuff there is. Look at the list of nutritional ingredients." He proudly handed the bag to Elizabeth.

Elizabeth studied the label. The names of the various ingredients didn't mean anything to her, but she could tell from the packaging that it was expensive.

"Ken, all this must have cost you a lot."

Ken shrugged. "I had some money saved up from mowing lawns."

Elizabeth peered inside the brown bag. There was something else in there. She reached in and took out a tube. "What's this?"

"It's medicine for his cuts," Ken said. "I got it from a veterinarian. It's supposed to help him heal faster." He took the tube from Elizabeth, opened it, and squeezed some cream onto his fingertip. Then, with a gentle touch, he began separating Joe's hair and rubbing the cream on his injuries. Joe barely flinched.

"You're wonderful with him," Elizabeth said with admiration.

Ken smiled. "I just think Joe is special."

Elizabeth took the dog food inside and emptied it into a bowl. Joe ate his gourmet food appreciatively, and afterwards Elizabeth and Ken tried to get him to play. They took turns rolling the ball at him. At first, Joe didn't know what to make of it. Then, with his nose, he began to roll it back to them.

"He's catching on!" Ken cried in delight.

Elizabeth got so caught up in the game she didn't hear Jessica come in through the gate.

"What are you doing home so early?" Elizabeth asked her. "I thought you were doing something with Lila and Ellen."

"I was, but I changed my mind." Jessica turned a little pink, and gave them an embarrassed smile. "I wanted to see how Joe was doing."

Elizabeth looked at her in amazement. Any dog that could win Jessica's heart had to be special.

Ken came home with the twins after school every day that week. As the days passed, Joe grew to trust them. He began meeting them at the gate, and following them around the yard. Ken found it easy to teach Joe to follow orders. Before long, the dog could sit, stand on his hind legs and beg, and stay still, whenever Ken told him. Joe liked Elizabeth and Jessica, too, but a real bond was forming between Joe and Ken.

On Thursday afternoon, they decided to give Joe another bath. This time Joe was a lot more frisky. Ken and Jessica had to hold him still while Elizabeth massaged the shampoo into his hair.

"That cream you put on his cuts really worked," Elizabeth noted. "The cuts are practically gone."

When she finished, Ken got the garden hose to rinse Joe off. He turned on the water and, remembering how Joe had reacted to the hose before, he approached the dog slowly.

This time, however, Joe didn't cringe at all. Instead, he leapt at the hose and grabbed it in his mouth, forcing the steady stream of water to change direction.

"Hey!" Jessica yelled in outrage as a blast of

water hit her in the face. Ken tried to get the hose away from him, but all the good food and exercise had made Joe a stronger dog. He held onto the hose, twisting and turning it. Before long, they were all drenched.

Elizabeth fell down on the ground, and doubled over with laughter. Ken was practically hysterical as he ran after Joe and the hose. Even Jessica was giggling now.

Elizabeth looked up and saw her parents standing on the porch, watching them. They were laughing, too. For a moment, she wondered how her parents would react if they knew what had really happened to Joe. But she and Jessica were determined to handle this situation by themselves.

Ken finally wrestled the hose away from Joe, but Joe was having too good a time to sit still and allow himself to be dried off. Next, he made them chase him around the yard with the towels.

Elizabeth paused at the back steps to catch her breath. Mrs. Wakefield was shaking her head in amusement. "Now you can see why I don't want a dog in the house."

Mr. Wakefield gazed out at the wet grass. "Well, the lawn probably needed watering anyway," he said, smiling. "You know, Elizabeth, I must admit I was wrong about you girls. I'm pleased with the way you two have handled your dog-walking business. You're showing very responsible behavior."

Elizabeth beamed. "Thanks, Dad."

"I hope you're sharing your profits with Ken," Mrs. Wakefield said. "He seems to be helping out a lot."

"He won't let us pay him," she told her parents. "I offered, but he refuses to take any money at all. He loves being with dogs, but his parents won't let him have one."

"That's too bad," her mother said, as she started back into the house. "He certainly has a way with animals."

"I hope he doesn't miss Joe too much when he leaves on Saturday," Mr. Wakefield added as he followed his wife inside.

Elizabeth's smile faded. Somehow, she'd managed to push aside the thought of Mr. Quincy's return until now. But it was already Thursday. In only two days, Mr. Quincy would be coming back for his dog. And then—what would happen to poor Joe?

Elizabeth wondered if this thought had occurred to the others. Joe had now allowed himself to be caught, and Ken and Jessica were rubbing him with the towels. Elizabeth joined them.

She picked up a brush, and began stroking Joe's fine white hair. "You know, Mr. Quincy will be coming back for Joe on Saturday."

Jessica shuddered. "That awful man."

Ken stroked Joe's head for a minute. Then in a firm and steady voice, he said, "We can't let Mr. Quincy get his hands on this dog. We have to think of a way to keep him from taking Joe back."

Seven

◇

Later that afternoon, Joe was peacefully taking a nap. Elizabeth fixed some snacks, and she and Jessica and Ken sat in the yard, eating and trying to think of what to do.

Elizabeth stroked the sleeping dog. "You're right," she told Ken. "We can't give Joe back to Mr. Quincy. He'll just start hurting him again."

"But how can we stop Mr. Quincy from taking him?" Jessica asked. "After all, Joe's *his* dog."

"Maybe we could tell the police," Elizabeth said thoughtfully.

"But how could we prove that Mr. Quincy's been hurting Joe?" Ken asked. "Like you said before, Elizabeth, the cuts have just about healed. There's very little evidence. I'm sure Mr. Quincy would deny everything, and it would be our word against his."

"Maybe we could tell Mr. Quincy that Joe ran away," Ken suggested.

"That's a good idea," Jessica said. "But where could we hide him?"

"What about the Sweet Valley Animal Shelter?" Elizabeth asked. "Maybe they could keep him there until we find a home for him."

Ken frowned. "The animal shelter would be the first place Mr. Quincy would look. He could identify Joe, and they'd give him right back."

"Wait a minute," Jessica said slowly. "What if he couldn't identify Joe?"

Elizabeth immediately recognized the gleam in Jessica's eyes. She'd seen that look before, and it usually meant that Jessica had some outrageous plan in mind.

Jessica jumped up. "I'll be right back." She ran into the house, and Ken turned to Elizabeth.

"What's going on?"

"I don't know," Elizabeth replied. "But I think she's got an idea."

Jessica flew back outside. "Look at this." She handed Elizabeth a bottle.

"Lady Beautiful Temporary Wash-In Hair Color," Elizabeth read. " 'Be the woman you dream of being.' Where'd you get this?"

Jessica giggled. "I bought it ages ago. I was thinking about dyeing my hair black."

Ken looked at her as if he thought she was nuts. "Why would you want to do something like that?"

"Just to be different," Jessica replied. "Sometimes, looking exactly like someone else can get boring. Anyway, I changed my mind and I didn't do it. I knew Mom and Dad would be furious."

"What does this have to do with Joe?" Elizabeth asked impatiently.

A slow grin began forming on Ken's face. "I think I've just figured out Jessica's scheme. We could dye Joe's hair!"

"Exactly!" Jessica exclaimed. "He'll look completely different. Even Mr. Quincy wouldn't recognize him."

Now Elizabeth started to get excited. "So if we have to take him to the animal shelter, and Mr. Quincy goes there looking for him—"

"He'll ask for a snow-white dog," Jessica burst in, "and they'll tell him there's no dog there who fits the description!"

Elizabeth gazed at her sister in admiration.

Jessica could be a pain sometimes, but she could also be brilliant!

Ken was examining the bottle. "I guess this stuff is safe."

"If it's good enough for people, it must be OK for dogs," Jessica assured him. "And it doesn't last forever. It washes out a little bit with each shampoo."

"Wait a minute," Ken said. "This stuff's meant for one head of hair. I don't think there's going to be enough for Joe."

"We could cut his hair," Jessica suggested. "That would make him look even more different."

Elizabeth fingered Joe's long, silky white hair regretfully. "It seems a shame . . . he's so beautiful."

"But it's worth sacrificing his looks if it means saving him from Mr. Quincy," Ken stated.

Joe began to stir from his nap. He opened his eyes, looked at Ken, and let out a short happy bark.

"What do you think, Joe?" Ken asked. "Would you mind being a short-haired black dog instead of a long-haired white one?"

Joe uttered another bark.

"Sounds like yes to me," Ken decided, grinning at the twins. "Have you got scissors?"

The cutting wasn't difficult. Joe stood obediently still while Jessica snipped at his hair. By the time they were finished, the grass was covered with strands of white hair.

"There!" Jessica put the scissors down. "How does he look?"

"Not bad," Elizabeth said politely. Actually, she thought poor Joe looked kind of bedraggled, but she didn't want to insult Jessica.

Ken was reading the directions on the hair coloring bottle. "This doesn't sound very difficult. First, we have to get him wet. You two hold him down while I get the hose."

Luckily, Joe seemed to be too tired from his earlier escapades to play with the hose again. Once he was wet, Jessica put on the plastic gloves, and proceeded to pour the contents of the bottle on Joe.

"Yuck," Elizabeth commented. "This stuff looks like slime. I can't believe you were going to put this stuff on your own hair, Jess."

"It'll look good when we're done," Jessica assured her. She began to smooth the gooky stuff all over Joe's body. Then she dabbed a little of the dye on Joe's face. "Some of the white is going to show, but I guess that's OK. He'll still look like a different dog."

The dye didn't seem to bother Joe at all. In

fact, as Jessica finished applying it, he fell asleep again. Jessica checked the bottle label. "Now we have to wait ten minutes before washing it off."

"Maybe I should call the animal shelter and find out if they'll take him," Elizabeth said.

Ken's forehead puckered. "I'm still not crazy about the idea of leaving him there, even for a short time. I'm sure they'd take good care of him, but Joe needs a lot of love. He needs a real home."

"Like yours," Elizabeth said softly.

Ken nodded.

Elizabeth had an inspiration. "You know, I'll bet if your parents could see you and Joe together, they'd understand how much he means to you. And then maybe they'd change their minds about letting you have a dog."

Ken looked at her hopefully. "Do you really think so?"

"It's worth trying," Elizabeth said. "Why don't we take Joe to your place after school tomorrow?"

"All right," Ken said eagerly.

"It's time!" Jessica announced. She picked up the hose. "Watch closely, you guys. You're about to see a brand-new Joe!"

On Friday afternoon, Elizabeth, Jessica, Ken,

and a very strange-looking dog headed toward the Matthews house.

"Well, you have to admit there's no way Mr. Quincy would recognize his dog," Jessica said.

The once beautiful animal was now—well, definitely not beautiful, Elizabeth thought. His hair was an assortment of colors—black in some patches, gray in others, with white spots around his eyes. The hair on one leg was much longer than the hair on the others.

"I wonder if he knows how funny he looks," Jessica said, giggling.

"Don't worry, Joe," Ken told the dog. "We still love you."

No one was home when they got to Ken's house. "I guess my mom's not back from work yet," he said. But just then, his mother's car pulled into the driveway.

"Hi, kids," Mrs. Matthews said. She joined them on the porch. "Whose dog is this?"

"No one's, really," Elizabeth lied. "We're just taking care of him until we can find him a home."

"Isn't he interesting looking?" Jessica asked.

Mrs. Matthews studied Joe with a bewildered look. "He's certainly—different."

"He's very sweet," Elizabeth told her.

"And obedient," Ken added.

"He hardly barks at all," Jessica offered.

Somehow, Joe seemed to understand what was going on. All on his own, he hopped up on his hind legs and lifted his front paws in a begging position.

Mrs. Matthews knew what was going on, too. She smiled at her son sadly. "Oh, Ken . . ."

"Mom, please? I promise I'll take good care of him. I'll be completely responsible. I'll feed him and walk him, and I'll never let him climb on the furniture."

"I'm sorry, Ken," his mother said, and she really did sound regretful. "We've been through this before, and you know how your father and I feel. Since both of us work, we don't have time to take care of a dog. And he would be such a large responsibility for you alone." She bent down and patted Joe's head. "Maybe next year you can get a dog."

"But I don't want just any dog," Ken pleaded. "I want Joe. He's special, Mom. He needs me. If you'd just give me a chance to prove I can take care of him—"

"I'm sorry, Ken," his mother said again. Her voice was sympathetic, but firm. "Now, why don't you kids stay out here and I'll bring you some lemonade and cookies?" As she opened the door, she glanced at her hand and frowned. "How did I get this black dye on my hand?"

"Uh-oh," Jessica whispered. "I guess we didn't get all that stuff out of his hair."

Ken sat down on the steps and hung his head. Joe curled up next to him. They both looked depressed.

"Now what are we going to do?" Jessica asked. "That terrible man is coming for him tomorrow. We have to find a home for him, fast."

"Let's think if any of our friends would like a dog," Elizabeth suggested.

Suddenly, Ken snapped his fingers. "I've got it!"

Before the girls could ask him what he meant, Mrs. Matthews reappeared with a tray bearing a pitcher of lemonade, glasses, and a plate of cookies.

"Mom," Ken said casually, "I was thinking about going out to visit Fred tomorrow. Is that OK?"

"I suppose so," his mother said. "I'll call him later and see if it's all right."

When she went back inside, Elizabeth asked, "Who's Fred?"

"He's my cousin," Ken told her. "He lives on a ranch about ten miles out of town. He's already got three dogs, and I'll bet he wouldn't mind having another."

"That's a great idea!" Jessica exclaimed. "Mr. Quincy will never find him if he's that far away."

"He'd have plenty of space, and other dogs to play with," Elizabeth noted.

"And I could visit him," Ken said. "You two want to come with me to bring him out there tomorrow?"

The twins nodded enthusiastically. "We'd better go early," Elizabeth warned. "We don't know what time Mr. Quincy is going to come for him."

Ken leaned over and hugged Joe. "I wish I could keep you, Joe. But you'll like Fred's ranch. And I promise I'll come out there every chance I can."

Then he got up, and Jessica immediately started giggling. Ken looked down at his T-shirt and groaned. His neat white shirt was streaked with black.

Eight

◇

"This place is fantastic!" Elizabeth exclaimed. She couldn't even guess at how many acres the ranch covered. It seemed to stretch out forever. In back of the house, there was a beautifully tended vegetable garden, and in the distance a grove of orange trees.

A ranch hand had met Elizabeth, Jessica, Ken, and Joe at the bus stop, and now they were outside the ranch house, waiting for Ken's cousin Fred.

"I'm sure he'll be here in a few minutes," the ranch hand told them. "He's tending the horses."

"Horses," Elizabeth murmured dreamily. "Ken,

this has to be the most perfect place in the world. Joe's going to love it here. Look at all the space he'll have to run around and play in."

Ken looked out over the area. "Yeah, it is pretty nice. What do you think, Joe?"

Joe barked appreciatively.

The ranch was so peaceful and lovely, Elizabeth felt like all their worries were just melting away. Only Jessica seemed to remember why they had come.

"I wonder what time Mr. Quincy's coming," she said. "He could be at our house right now. I hope he's gone before we get home."

Elizabeth shook her head. "I don't. I mean, we should be there when he comes. It's not fair to leave Mom and Dad to deal with him alone. They won't know what's going on."

"I guess he'll be pretty angry when he finds Joe gone," Jessica commented.

"That guy's mean-looking even when he's not angry," Ken said.

Elizabeth felt pangs of guilt as she imagined her parents having to deal with an irate Mr. Quincy. "I wish we could hang around here, but I really think we should be home before he comes. What are we going to say to him about Joe?"

"We'll say he ran away," Jessica replied. "There's no way Mr. Quincy can prove he didn't."

Elizabeth felt uncomfortable at the thought of lying, especially in front of her parents.

But then she looked at Joe. Even though his physical appearance was pretty peculiar, his cuts had healed, and he was acting like a normal dog. Maybe it was worth lying to see him so happy.

"Here comes Fred now," Ken announced.

A lanky man in jeans and a denim jacket strode toward them. He was accompanied by two German shepherds, one on either side of him. Each dog appeared to compete for Fred's attention by barking louder than the other.

"How are you doing, Ken?" Fred asked, throwing an arm around Ken's shoulders.

"Pretty good," Ken said. "These are my friends, Elizabeth and Jessica Wakefield."

Fred shook hands with the twins, and then bent down to look at Joe. "And who's this?"

"This is Joe," Ken said. "Shake hands, Joe." This was Joe's most recent trick.

Joe obligingly lifted his right front paw and Fred shook it.

"So you finally talked your parents into letting you have a dog," Fred noted.

"No," Ken said dolefully. "We, uh, we found

Joe, and, um, he doesn't have a home. I wanted to keep him but Mom and Dad won't let me. He's a great dog, Fred, and he really needs a home."

Fred looked a little mystified as he ruffled Joe's fur. "Whoever had him before must have been a little strange."

Elizabeth was surprised to hear him say this. She thought all Joe's signs of abuse had disappeared.

"Someone did something crazy to his hair," Fred continued. "It looks like it's been dyed. And whoever chopped it off like this isn't much of a groomer."

Out of the corner of her eye, Elizabeth could see her sister turn a little pink. "I think he's in good health, though," she said hastily.

"And he's got a great personality," Ken added. "He's really smart, too, and obedient."

Fred grinned at him. "Are you leading up to asking me something?"

Ken smiled back. "Yeah. I was wondering if maybe you'd like to keep him. I'm really crazy about this dog. I'd like him to be someplace where I know he'll be treated well, and where I can visit him."

Fred stroked Joe's head. Joe looked up and licked Fred's hand. *How could anyone not want such a loving dog*, Elizabeth thought. She was going to miss Joe. And she knew this was really hard on Ken.

"He seems like a good dog," Fred said. "Very alert and affectionate."

"Then you'll keep him?" Ken asked eagerly.

"Sure," Fred replied. "As long as he gets along with George and Harry."

The two German shepherds had stopped barking, and they were eyeing Joe. Joe moved toward them, and Fred's dogs began circling him. Elizabeth held her breath. What if they started fighting? Fred would never keep Joe then.

The dogs began sniffing each other. Then one of the German shepherds nuzzled Joe's neck.

"Let's leave them alone for a little while and see how they get along," Fred said. "You kids come on inside the house and I'll whip up some breakfast. How do blueberry pancakes sound to you?"

Elizabeth looked at her watch. The thought of Mr. Quincy showing up before they got home made her uneasy. "We really should be getting back," she started to say, but Jessica interrupted her.

"I *love* blueberry pancakes! And I'm absolutely starving!"

Ken echoed her sentiments, so Elizabeth was

overruled. And she had to admit she wasn't all that eager to face Mr. Quincy either.

"Where'd you find Joe?" Fred asked as they went into the house.

"Oh, he just sort of wandered into the twins' back yard," Ken said vaguely. *Well*, Elizabeth thought, *at least that's not a total lie.*

After a hearty breakfast, during which Elizabeth asked numerous questions about Fred's horses, they went back outside. The dogs seemed to be getting along beautifully.

"It looks like Joe's found himself a home," Fred told Ken.

"Thanks, Fred," Ken said with great relief. "I know he'll be happy here."

"Want to have a look at my horses?" Fred asked Elizabeth.

Elizabeth gazed wistfully in the direction of the corral, but she shook her head. "We have to get back," she said, throwing Jessica and Ken a meaningful look. "We've got somebody to see back home."

"Well, come back any time," Fred told her. "And I hope I'll be seeing a lot of you, Ken, now that Joe's here."

Watching Joe play, Ken's face was a mixture of emotions. There was pleasure at seeing him so happy, but there was pain at the thought of leaving him. Just then, Joe spotted Ken, and came bounding over. Ken went down on his knees and threw his arms around the dog's neck.

"I'll miss you, Joe. And I'll be thinking about you all the time."

Elizabeth's and Jessica's eyes both grew tearful as they watched Ken say goodbye to Joe.

The bus ride back was quiet. Ken was depressed. Elizabeth couldn't stop wondering what they'd find when they got home.

"Maybe he'll be glad," Jessica said suddenly.

"What?" Elizabeth asked.

"Maybe Mr. Quincy will be glad to find out that Joe's gone," Jessica explained. "If he abused Joe, he couldn't have liked him very much."

What Jessica was suggesting made sense to Elizabeth, but she had a feeling Mr. Quincy wouldn't be sharing their viewpoint.

"Want me to go home with you?" Ken asked when they got off the bus just a few blocks from the Wakefields' home.

Jessica and Elizabeth nodded gratefully, and the three started up the street. Jessica was still feeling optimistic. "Maybe he's not even coming. Maybe he's forgotten all about Joe."

"Maybe he never even intended to come back,"

Ken offered. "Maybe he left Joe at your house to get rid of him."

But when they turned the corner to their block, all hopes vanished. The black sports car was parked at the curb right in front of their house.

"Let's not panic," Elizabeth managed to say. "We're all in this together."

Bracing themselves, the three went into the house.

The Wakefields were sitting in the living room while Mr. Quincy paced impatiently.

"There you are!" Mrs. Wakefield jumped up when she saw them. "We were getting worried about you!"

"I told Mr. Quincy you were probably taking Joe for a walk," Mr. Wakefield said.

"Where is he?" Mr. Quincy demanded.

Elizabeth couldn't bear to look at the man's beady eyes. She studied his feet as she spoke. "We don't know."

"What?"

Elizabeth looked at Jessica in desperation. Jessica was so much better at lying than she was.

And Jessica didn't fail her. She faced Mr. Quincy directly, her eyes wide and innocent. "When we went out to feed him this morning, he was gone! We've been looking for him all day."

For a second, Mr. Quincy was speechless.

"This is outrageous!" he yelled finally. "How could something like that happen?"

Mr. Wakefield calmly questioned the twins. "How *did* this happen, girls?"

Ken stepped forward. "It was my fault. When I was here yesterday afternoon, I think I may have left the gate open."

"It's not your fault," Elizabeth said, not wanting Ken to be blamed.

"It certainly is not," their father said sternly. "You girls were responsible for that dog, not Ken."

"I don't care whose fault it was," Mr. Quincy fumed. "I want my dog back. I should have known better than to trust a couple of irresponsible children!" His face was now purple with rage, and Elizabeth looked away.

She was equally angry that Mr. Quincy had the nerve to demand back a dog he intentionally mistreated.

"And why aren't you out looking for him right now?" Mr. Quincy demanded.

"We've been searching for hours!" Jessica replied.

"That's not enough!" Mr. Quincy declared.

Mr. Wakefield was looking grim. "He's right. Let's go in the car now and have a look around."

Jessica and Elizabeth and Ken looked at each other, but didn't say anything. They followed Mr. Wakefield out of the house. As they were leaving, Elizabeth heard her mother offering Mr. Quincy some coffee.

"I don't want any coffee! I want my dog back!"

She felt bad leaving her mother alone with such an awful man. And she felt even worse knowing they were out looking for a dog that would never be found.

Jessica and Ken sat in the backseat, and Elizabeth rode up front with her father. She stared out the window, pretending to be looking for Joe. She could tell her father was terribly upset and disappointed with them.

They drove in silence, up and down the streets of Sweet Valley. At one point, Mr. Wakefield caught a glimpse of a white dog behind a tree, and got out to look at him. Of course, it wasn't Joe.

After almost an hour, they returned home. Mr. Wakefield got out of the car, shaking his head angrily. "That dog could be anywhere. He could be halfway to Los Angeles by now. He could be lying in a street, injured. Do you kids understand how serious this is?"

Without waiting for an answer, he walked ahead of them into the house.

Elizabeth looked at the others miserably. "I wish we could tell them what really happened."

"But we can't," Jessica insisted. "Dad would only go out to the ranch and get Joe and bring him back to Mr. Quincy."

"Think about Joe," Ken pleaded to Elizabeth. "If he goes back to Mr. Quincy, you know what will happen to him."

Elizabeth couldn't bear the thought of that man abusing Joe. As much as she wanted to tell her parents the truth, she knew that she couldn't risk Joe's well-being.

They started back to the house, and almost collided with Mr. Quincy, who was storming out.

"I want that dog found!" he yelled through the door at the Wakefields. "And if he's not, you'll be hearing from my lawyers!"

He didn't say a word to the kids. He just shot one furious glance at them and walked rapidly to his car.

They watched in silence as he drove away.

"Gee, do you think he'll actually sue us?" Ken asked.

"Not us," Elizabeth replied unhappily. "Our parents."

Ken looked at them earnestly. "I'm sorry about

this. I feel like I'm the one who talked you into hiding Joe."

Elizabeth assured him it wasn't his fault. "We made this decision together."

"I guess this means we're not going to get that twenty dollars," Jessica said.

Elizabeth had completely forgotten about the twenty dollars they were supposed to get when Mr. Quincy returned. Of course, he wouldn't be paying them now. They'd probably even have to give back the twenty dollars he'd given them when he dropped Joe off.

Now, on top of everything else, they wouldn't even get to go to Sandy Harbor.

Nine

◇

When Elizabeth woke up the next morning, the weather matched her mood: The sky was gray and cloudy.

The evening before, she and Jessica had heard a long lecture from their parents about trust, responsibility, and maturity. They'd listened silently as their parents scolded them for their carelessness and expressed extreme disappointment in their behavior.

Elizabeth dragged herself out of bed and pulled on some jeans and a T-shirt. She had just come out of her room when the phone rang.

"Hello?"

"Elizabeth, it's Ken." His voice sounded rushed and nervous.

"Ken, what's wrong?"

"My cousin Fred just called me. You're not going to believe what happened. Fred said Joe was gone this morning. He's run away from the ranch!"

"Oh no!" Elizabeth's head was swimming. Another calamity was all that they needed. "What are you going to do?"

"I have to go out to the ranch and help search for him. Can you and Jessica come, too?"

Luckily, their parents hadn't grounded them. "We'll be right over," Elizabeth promised.

She hung up and ran into Jessica's room.

"Jess, wake up and get dressed! It's an emergency!"

Jessica opened one eye. "I *am* awake. I'm just dreaming about Sandy Harbor—and how we're not going."

"Forget Sandy Harbor," Elizabeth ordered. "We've got something more important to think about." Quickly, she relayed Ken's message.

Thirty minutes later, the twins were ringing Ken's doorbell. When Ken opened the door and came out, Elizabeth immediately noticed how distressed Ken was. Things had gone from bad to worse.

"My parents won't let me go to the ranch," he told them miserably.

"Why not?" Jessica asked.

"Because I was just there yesterday. They said that's enough for one weekend."

Elizabeth felt totally helpless. "I don't understand all this. Why did Joe run away? He looked so happy there." No one had any answer.

Jessica looked up at the sky. "I think it's going to rain." No sooner had she spoken than large drops began to fall. Soon it was pouring.

"Joe's out in this rain," Ken said sadly. "He must be getting soaked."

Elizabeth tried to comfort him. "Maybe he's found shelter. Maybe he's under a tree somewhere."

Ken's expression became even gloomier. "But what if there's a real storm? What if there's thunder and lightning? What if the lightning hits a tree? What if—"

"Ken!" Elizabeth couldn't bear to hear anymore. "Listen, you two, we can't just hang around here worrying about him. We've got to do something."

"Well, I'm not going out in this rain to look for him," Jessica said. "Besides, that ranch is ten miles away. Joe could be anywhere."

"There's only one thing we can do," Elizabeth stated flatly. She knew they weren't going to like what she was about to say. But like it or not, it was their only option. "We have to confess. We have to go home and tell Mom and Dad what really happened."

"What good will that do?" Ken asked.

"I don't know," Elizabeth said honestly. "But we have to tell them everything; that Mr. Quincy abused Joe and how we tried to save him. Maybe Dad will take us out to look for him again."

"They're going to be really angry when they find out we lied to them," Jessica noted.

"Look, we can't get into any more trouble than we're already in," Elizabeth argued.

There was a moment of silence as Jessica and Ken contemplated this.

"All right," Ken said finally, and Jessica nodded too.

The rain had eased a bit, but it was still sprinkling. Huddled under one umbrella, the kids ran back to the Wakefields' house. When they walked in the front door, they heard a familiar bark. And suddenly, Joe was bounding toward them.

He leaped on Ken and began licking his face. "Joe! Where did you come from?"

Elizabeth and Jessica watched in amazement. The rain had washed away Joe's dye, and he was white again. How had he found his way back? Joe was even smarter than they had thought.

Their elation didn't last very long, though. Mr. and Mrs. Wakefield walked into the room, and their expressions were serious.

"Joe showed up here just after you left," Mr. Wakefield informed them. "You kids are very, very lucky. I don't think Mr. Quincy was kidding when he talked about a lawsuit."

"Mr. Quincy?" Elizabeth repeated faintly.

Mrs. Wakefield nodded. "We just called him to tell him Joe's back. He's on his way over here right now."

"No!" Ken cried out in anguish. "You can't let him take Joe away! You can't!"

Mrs. Wakefield looked very concerned, and put an arm around Ken's shoulder. "Ken, I know you've become very attached to Joe, but he *is* Mr. Quincy's dog. I'm afraid there's nothing you can do about that."

"You don't understand!" Elizabeth exclaimed. But before she could say any more, there was a knock on the door. Mr. Wakefield went to answer it, and returned with Mr. Quincy.

"So, you found him," Mr. Quincy said with grim satisfaction. "You can forget about getting that additional twenty dollars, however. After the care, or lack of care, you've shown this dog, you're fortunate I don't ask for my original twenty dollars back."

No one was listening to him. Everyone was looking at Joe. With fear in his eyes, Joe whimpered and cowered behind Ken, his head bowed down.

"Your dog doesn't seemed thrilled to see you," Mr. Wakefield commented.

"Never mind that," Mr. Quincy snapped. "Joe! Get over here!"

But Joe didn't budge. Ken knelt down beside him, and held him tightly.

"Let go of my dog!" Mr. Quincy yelled.

"No!" Ken declared, loudly and strongly. "You're not taking this dog away!"

"Ken!" Mrs. Wakefield exclaimed.

"Mrs. Wakefield, he was abusing Joe. We can't let him take Joe back. He'll just start hurting him again!"

Elizabeth watched Mr. Quincy's reaction to this accusation. The man looked stunned at first, and then noticeably nervous. He stepped back, and eyed Ken warily.

Mr. Wakefield was watching him, too. "Is this true, Mr. Quincy?"

Mr. Quincy made an attempt to recover his

confidence. "That's an outrageous lie! Now release my dog."

"Ken's not lying, Dad," Elizabeth declared. "I saw the cuts."

"So did I," Jessica added.

"And look how scared he is of Mr. Quincy," Elizabeth went on.

"I could show you the bruises, Mr. Wakefield," Ken offered, still clinging to Joe.

Elizabeth looked at Ken in alarm. Didn't he remember that the wounds had all healed?

Mr. Wakefield took a step toward Joe, but he didn't get very far. Mr. Quincy rushed toward the dog and attempted to forcibly pull him away from Ken. Joe howled pitifully.

"Stop it!" Mr. Wakefield ordered, and Elizabeth practically jumped. She'd never heard her father speak so harshly. "I suspect that what Ken and the girls are telling me is true, Mr. Quincy. And dog abuse is against the law. If you take that dog away, I'll press charges against you."

Mr. Quincy quickly removed his hands from Joe and backed away. The room was charged with tension as he glared at Mr. Wakefield.

When Mr. Quincy finally spoke, his tone was disdainful. "Of course, the child is lying. But keep the dog, I don't care. He was costing me too much in dog food anyway."

"I hope you won't attempt to get another dog," Mr. Wakefield said. "Because if I ever see you with one, I'll start an investigation."

"Don't worry, I never want to see another dog," the man snapped. With that, he turned abruptly and walked out.

Elizabeth ran to her father and threw her arms around him. "Thank you, Dad. You just saved Joe's life."

"You're welcome," Mr. Wakefield said, but he looked a little confused.

"That was a good bluff, Ken," Jessica said.

"What do you mean, a good bluff?" Mrs. Wakefield asked. She looked alarmed. "Kids, you weren't lying about Joe being abused, were you?"

"Oh, no, Mrs. Wakefield," Ken assured her. "But you see, we treated the cuts and bruises with medicated cream. And they're all healed now."

"I still don't understand," Mr. Wakefield said. "If you kids were so concerned about this dog, why were you so careless with him?"

"We weren't careless," Elizabeth said. "We just didn't know what else to tell Mr. Quincy."

Mr. Wakefield rubbed his forehead. "I think I'm missing something here."

"Me, too," Mrs. Wakefield agreed. "Would you kids like to tell us the whole story? From the beginning?"

"I guess it's safe now," Ken said.

Elizabeth nodded happily. Admitting the truth was going to make her feel a lot better than she'd felt in days.

"Sure," she said to her parents. "Here goes."

"Hold on!" Ken called to Elizabeth. He was looking out the front window. "Here come my parents. I think we might as well tell them the whole story, too."

Mrs. Wakefield opened the door and greeted Mr. and Mrs. Matthews. "We're just about to hear what these kids of ours have been up to," she told them.

"Good!" Mrs. Matthews exclaimed. "Ken's cousin Fred just called to tell him they haven't found the dog. *What* dog? Is he talking about the dog you brought home the other day, Ken? What was he doing at Fred's?"

"Is this the dog?" Mr. Matthews asked, pointing at Joe.

Ken nodded, and his mother looked puzzled. "But he was a different color the other day, wasn't he?"

"How about letting us in on what's been going on?" Mr. Matthews suggested.

Elizabeth began again. "When Mr. Quincy brought Joe, we thought the dog acted awfully strange. Every time we went near him, he cringed, as if he were afraid of us. Then, we were giving him a bath when Ken discovered something."

"There were cuts and bruises all over his body," Ken said. "I could tell he'd been abused."

"Ken got medication for Joe's cuts," Elizabeth said. "And he came to see Joe every day, playing with him and getting him to trust us."

"We didn't want to give him back to Mr. Quincy because we knew what that awful man would do to him," Ken told them.

Jessica took over. "So I suggested we disguise him so Mr. Quincy couldn't recognize him. So we cut his hair and dyed it."

"We had to find a place to hide him," Ken said. "That was why I brought him home, Mom and Dad. But you said I couldn't keep him."

Mr. and Mrs. Matthews exchanged looks.

"Then we took him to Fred's ranch," Ken continued. "But he ran away and came back here."

"Wait a minute," Mr. Wakefield said. "Jessica, Elizabeth, why didn't you tell us about the dog being abused when you first discovered it?"

"Because you said you didn't want to hear us complaining about our job," Elizabeth explained.

"We figured we'd better work this out by ourselves, to show you how responsible we are."

Her father sighed. "Elizabeth, when I said no complaining, I meant about things like feeding the dogs, or bathing them. You should always come to us with important problems like this."

"That dog's life was in danger," Mrs. Wakefield said. "We could have helped you."

"But you might not have believed us," Ken objected.

"What do you mean?" Mrs. Matthews asked.

"Well, I keep telling you I'm old enough to take care of a dog. But you don't believe me."

Mr. and Mrs. Matthews looked at each other again. "Oh, Ken," Mrs. Matthews said sadly. "I'm sorry. I guess we still think of you as a little boy."

Mr. Matthews nodded. "I think we've underestimated you. You worked very hard to save this dog's life. I'm very impressed."

"We're proud of you girls, too," Mr. Wakefield said. "I still believe you should have told us about Joe's problems, but overall I think you behaved in a very grown-up manner."

The twins looked at each other and beamed. "Thanks, Dad," Elizabeth said. "I didn't want to lie to you. But we thought it was our job to help Joe."

"And now he's safe from that terrible Mr. Quincy," Ken said. He was sitting on the floor, with Joe's head in his lap. "Poor Joe. You've had a rough day, haven't you?"

"What are we going to do about Joe?" Elizabeth asked. "He still needs a good home."

Ken's father whispered something in Mrs. Matthews's ear, and she nodded. "He's got one," Mr. Matthews said.

Ken looked up, his face registering disbelief. "You mean—I can keep him?"

His parents nodded. "You hear that, buddy? You're coming home with me!" Ken excitedly announced to Joe.

Joe looked up and uttered one short bark. Ken hugged him, and then leaped up to hug his parents.

"I think this calls for a celebration," Mrs. Wakefield said. "Jessica, could you help me in the kitchen?"

They reappeared a few minutes later with a cake Mrs. Wakefield had baked that morning. As she was cutting it, Steven appeared. He seemed to have a sixth sense that lured him toward good food.

Elizabeth accepted a slice of cake from her mother and smiled. "Now everything's perfect," she said.

"*Almost* perfect," Jessica reminded her. "We still don't have the money to go to Sandy Harbor, remember?"

"That's right," Elizabeth sighed. In her happiness at seeing Joe safe, she had forgotten all about their trip.

"How much more do you need?" Mrs. Wakefield asked.

"Twenty dollars," Jessica told her. "That's what Mr. Quincy was supposed to pay us when he picked Joe up."

Mr. Wakefield reached into his pocket and pulled out his wallet. "Well, I think saving a dog's life is worth a reward, don't you?"

Mrs. Wakefield nodded. "How much do you think the reward should be?"

Mr. Wakefield pretended to be thinking seriously. "How does twenty dollars sound to you?"

"Perfect!" Mrs. Wakefield declared.

Elizabeth clapped her hands while Jessica let out a cheer.

"This is fantastic!" Ken exclaimed. "I get Joe, you guys get to go on your trip—now everybody's happy!"

"Wait a minute," Steven said, and he looked at the twins pointedly. "Aren't you forgetting something?"

Jessica groaned. "Oh, yeah, that's right." She turned to her father. "We borrowed five dollars from Steven to make the flyers for our dog-walking business."

"Well, I suppose the reward could include covering your debts," Mr. Wakefield said, and reached for his wallet again.

"Don't forget the interest," Steven added.

Mr. Wakefield eyed his son suspiciously. "How much interest?"

Steven didn't seem quite willing to meet his father's eyes. "Fifty percent. So they actually owe me seven dollars and fifty cents."

Mrs. Wakefield looked at him in amazement. "You charged your own sisters fifty percent interest?"

Steven shrugged nonchalantly. "Well, I heard you tell them you wanted them to learn the value of money."

Mr. Wakefield rolled his eyes and shook his head. "What *have* you learned about the value of money, girls?"

Jessica grinned. "It's a lot easier to spend than it is to earn!"

Elizabeth nodded fervently. "And I know we'll appreciate our trip to Sandy Harbor—because we've definitely earned it!"

* * *

A few days later, Amy Sutton came home with Elizabeth after school. "Did you realize March is almost over, Elizabeth?" Amy asked as they settled down in the den with a plateful of cookies and two big glasses of milk. "And you know what *that* means." She took a sip of milk. "April Fools' Day! I'm going to come up with something really wild this year."

"Like what?" Elizabeth asked.

"I haven't decided yet," Amy admitted. "But it'll be great! Just wait and see."

Elizabeth smiled. "Do you remember last year when Ms. Applebaum called a surprise quiz and made us take the whole test before she let us know it was an April Fools' joke?"

"I didn't think it was very funny. I panicked. Well, what are you going to do this year, Elizabeth? You're not switching identities with Jessica again, are you?"

"Probably," Elizabeth answered.

Amy made a face. "But that's what you did last year. And the year before that."

Elizabeth giggled. "I know. It's sort of a tradition. And we do always manage to fool someone."

Just then Jessica stuck her head in the room. "Hi! What are you guys doing?"

"Talking about April Fools' Day," Elizabeth told her.

Jessica grinned. "Oh, yeah? I've been thinking about it, too, and I've got a great idea for us this year, Lizzie. It's much better than what we usually do. Wait till you hear it. It's absolutely, positively fantastic! We'll fool everyone."

What kind of fantastic scheme does Jessica have up her sleeve for April Fools' Day? Find out in Sweet Valley Twins #28, APRIL FOOL!